P9-CBR-202

7/08

TULSA CITY-COUNTY LIBRARY

A Note to Parents and Caregivers:

Read-it! Readers are for children who are just starting on the amazing road to reading. These beautiful books support both the acquisition of reading skills and the love of books.

 The PURPLE LEVEL presents basic topics and objects using high frequency words and simple language patterns.

 The RED LEVEL presents familiar topics using common words and repeating sentence patterns.

 The BLUE LEVEL presents new ideas using a larger vocabulary and varied sentence structure.

 The YELLOW LEVEL presents more challenging ideas, a broad vocabulary, and wide variety in sentence structure.

 The GREEN LEVEL presents more complex ideas, an extended vocabulary range, and expanded language structures.

 The ORANGE LEVEL presents a wide range of ideas and concepts using challenging vocabulary and complex language structures.

When sharing a book with your child, read in short stretches, pausing often to talk about the pictures. Have your child turn the pages and point to the pictures and familiar words. And be sure to reread favorite stories or parts of stories.

There is no right or wrong way to share books with children. Find time to read with your child, and pass on the legacy of literacy.

Adria F. Klein, Ph.D.
Professor Emeritus
California State University
San Bernardino, California

Editor: Nick Healy
Designer: Amy Muehlenhardt
Page Production: Lori Bye
Creative Director: Keith Griffin
Editorial Director: Carol Jones
The illustrations in this book were created digitally.

Picture Window Books
5115 Excelsior Boulevard
Suite 232
Minneapolis, MN 55416
877-845-8392
www.picturewindowbooks.com

Copyright © 2007 by Picture Window Books
All rights reserved. No part of this book may be reproduced without written
permission from the publisher. The publisher takes no responsibility for the use of
any of the materials or methods described in this book, nor for the products thereof.

Printed in the United States of America.

Library of Congress Cataloging-in-Publication Data
Blackaby, Susan.
Tricky twins / by Susan Blackaby ; illustrated by Len Epstein.
p. cm. — (Read-it! readers)
Summary: Ricky and Nicky are twins, and even though they are like two peas in a
pod, it is not as hard to tell them apart as it could be.
ISBN-13: 978-1-4048-2419-5 (hardcover)
ISBN-10: 1-4048-2419-7 (hardcover)
[1. Twins—Fiction. 2. Brothers and sisters—Fiction. 3. Clothing and dress—
Fiction. 4. Asian Americans—Fiction.] I. Epstein, Len, ill. II. Title. III. Series.

PZ7.B5318Tre 2006
[E]—dc22   2006003392

Tricky Twins

by Susan Blackaby

illustrated by Len Epstein

Special thanks to our advisers for their expertise:

Adria F. Klein, Ph.D.
Professor Emeritus, California State University
San Bernardino, California

Susan Kesselring, M.A.
Literacy Educator
Rosemount–Apple Valley–Eagan (Minnesota) School District

PICTURE WINDOW BOOKS
Minneapolis, Minnesota

Ricky and Nicky are twins. They are like two peas in a pod.

They both have black hair. They both have dark eyes.

Ricky and Nicky like to wear clothes that match.

Ricky has red shoes. Nicky has red shoes, too.

11

Ricky has purple socks. Nicky has purple socks, too.

Ricky wears blue jeans.

Nicky wears blue jeans, too.

Ricky wears a brown belt with a gold buckle. Nicky wears a brown belt with a gold buckle, too.

Ricky likes stripes. He has a striped shirt. Nicky likes stripes, too.

The twins have matching
hooded jackets.

21

You might think it is hard to tell the twins apart. But it isn't always.

More *Read-it!* Readers

Bright pictures and fun stories help you practice your reading skills. Look for more books at your level.

Ann Plants a Garden 1-4048-1010-2

The Babysitter 1-4048-1187-7

Bess and Tess 1-4048-1013-7

The Best Soccer Player 1-4048-1055-2

Dan Gets Set 1-4048-1011-0

Fishing Trip 1-4048-1004-8

Jen Plays 1-4048-1008-0

Joey's First Day 1-4048-1174-5

Just Try It 1-4048-1175-3

Mary's Art 1-4048-1056-0

The Missing Tooth 1-4048-1592-9

Moving Day 1-4048-1006-4

Pat Picks Up 1-4048-1059-5

A Place for Mike 1-4048-1012-9

Room to Share 1-4048-1185-0

Shopping for Lunch 1-4048-1589-9

Syd's Room 1-4048-1585-6

Wes Gets a Pet 1-4048-1060-9

Winter Fun for Kat 1-4048-1007-2

A Year of Fun 1-4048-1009-9

Looking for a specific title or level? A complete list of *Read-it!* Readers is available on our Web site:

www.picturewindowbooks.com